Flippity Floppity

By
Stephen Cosgrove

Illustrated by
Merry Ann McGlinn

IDEALS CHILDREN'S BOOKS

Nashville, Tennessee

Published by Ideals Publishing Corporation
Nelson Place at Elm Hill Pike
Nashville, TN 37214

ISBN 0-8249-8321-1

Dedicated to all little bunnies who have to hippity-hoppity, flippity-floppity off to bed.
Stephen

Under a rainbow, in a forest far away, there lived a fat little bunny who played all day.

He was a funny, happy bunny, who giggled
and laughed when anyone tickled his tummy.

His name was Flippity, but the others called him
Floppity because of the funny way that he hopped.
For, you see, his ears kind of flipped and
flopped as he hopped.

Look! There he goes now, hop, hop, hopping along as he sings his little song!

One day, Flippity Floppity hopped over to
the meadow for his lunch.

There, he sat down and munched with a
Scrunch! Scrunch! Cruuunch!

After Floppity finished his munching, he felt a bit tired from all of his lunching.

So, he stretched a big stretch and
he yawned a big yawn.

And just like that, he disappeared. He
was gone!

Oh, no! Where did Floppity go?

Look out, little bunny! Don't run into that crow!

There he goes, hippity-hoppity, as his feet go cloppity and his ears go floppity.

Look at him run. This way, then that way.
Nothing can stop this bunny today.

Floppity even leaped over the frog-hoppers,
who sat beside the creek filled with fish-floppers.

Flippity Floppity had to hop home for a nap,
it was said.

But not until his favorite story was read.

Shhh... Shhh...
Flippity Floppity is cuddled so deep.

Shhh... Shhh...
Flippity Floppity is fast asleep.

About the Author

In 1973 Stephen Cosgrove stumbled into a bookstore to buy a fantasy book for his daughter but couldn't find one that he really liked. He decided he was looking for something that hadn't been written. "I went home and that night I wrote my first book."

Since that fledgling effort over a decade ago, Cosgrove's books have sold millions of copies worldwide.

Cosgrove was born in 1945. He attended Stephens College for Women in Columbia, Missouri ("A great year but I learned little and forgot a lot"), is married, and lives on a quiet, little farm in Washington. There he writes on his computer, communicates by telefax with eight children's book illustrators about current projects, and takes healthy breaks to play with the dog and pick the daisies.